Scat, Cats!

by JOAN HOLUB

illustrated by RICH DAVIS

VIKING

VIKING
Published by the Penguin Group
Penguin Putnam Books for Young Readers, 345 Hudson Street, New York, New York 10014, U.S.A.
Penguin Books Ltd, 27 Wrights Lane, London W8 5TZ, England
Penguin Books Australia Ltd, Ringwood, Victoria, Australia
Penguin Books Canada Ltd, 10 Alcorn Avenue, Toronto, Ontario, Canada M4V 3B2
Penguin Books (N.Z.) Ltd, 182-190 Wairau Road, Auckland 10, New Zealand

Penguin Books Ltd, Registered Offices: Harmondsworth, Middlesex, England

First published by Viking and Puffin Books,
divisions of Penguin Putnam Books for Young Readers, 2001

5 7 9 10 8 6 4

LIBRARY OF CONGRESS CATALOGING-IN-PUBLICATION DATA
Holub, Joan.
Scat cats! / by Joan Holub ; illustrated by Rich Davis.
p. cm.
Summary: Cats cause so much trouble in a house that they are
shooed away—and then missed!
ISBN 0-670-89279-3 (hardcover) — ISBN 0-14-130905-9 (pbk.)
[1. Cats–Fiction. 2. Stories in rhyme.] I. Davis, Rich, 1958– ill. II. Title.
PZ8.3.H74 Sc 2001 [E]—dc21 00-010967

Viking® and Easy-to-Read® are registered trademarks of Penguin Putnam Inc.

Printed in Hong Kong

Reading Level 1.9

For my sister Kristen,
who never met a cat she didn't like.—J.H.

To Peter, my brother and best friend.
Thank you for all the ways you've been
there for me. I greatly admire the
wonderful creative gift God has given you
and believe that the best is yet to be!
We won't forget Powacket...—R.D.

Scat, cats! Go away!

Shoo, cats! You can't stay.

You, cats? Back again?

No, cats. Don't come in!

Fast cats sneak inside.

Striped cats try to hide.

Bad cats trip my feet.

Loud cats want to eat.

Pest cats claw the chair.

Wild cats everywhere.

Quick cats dash on by.

Sly cats jump up high.

Show-off cats try to zoom.

Kersplat! Crash! Bang! Boom!

Stop, cats! No! No! No!

Out, cats. Out you go!

No cats at our door.

No cats anymore.

No cats come to play.

No cats. Where are they?

Here, cats! Hey! Yoo-hoo!

Dear cats, we miss you!

Look! Look!

A cat track!

Cats! Cats!

You came back!

Nice cats, come on in.

Oh, cats! Where have you been?

Here, cats. Have some chow.

Glad cats say, "Meow."

Warm cats in our laps.

Sweet cats take their naps.

Fat cats purr all day.

Our cats. Here to stay.